THE
WHALE THAT FELL
WITH A SUBMA

Akiyuki Nosaka

illustrated by Mika Provata-Carlone

translated from the Japanese by Ginny Tapley Takemori

PUSHKIN CHILDREN'S BOOKS

Pushkin Children's Books
71–75 Shelton Street
London, WC2H 9JQ

The Whale That Fell in Love with a Submarine first published in Japanese as 戦争童話集
(*Sensō dōwa shū*) in 2003 by Chuokoron-Shinsha, Inc., Tokyo (Original edition 1980)

English language translation rights arranged with Akiyuki Nosaka through Japan Foreign-Rights Centre

Original text © 2003 Akiyuki Nosaka
Illustrations © 2015 Mika Provata-Carlone

English translation © Ginny Tapley Takemori 2015
This translation first published by Pushkin Press in 2015

The verses quoted in 'The Parrot and the Boy' are from the song 'Seagull Sailors' by Toshiko Takeuchi, translated by B. Ito

ISBN 978 1 782690 27 6

Text designed and typeset by Tetragon, London

Printed in China by WKT Co

www.pushkinchildrens.com

On 15th August 1945, Emperor Hirohito gave a recorded radio address across Japan, in which he announced the surrender of Japan to the Allies. As such, it is considered the day the war ended, and is celebrated each year in Japan as the National Memorial Service for War Dead.

Since 1982, it is also known as "The day for mourning of war dead and praying for peace" (戦歿者を追悼し平和を祈念する). It is also when many regions celebrate the traditional Obon festival of Japan to honour their ancestors.

Contents

The Whale That
Fell in Love with a Submarine

South-south-east of the Izu Islands, off the coast of a small islet, there was a whale.

He wasn't swimming or blowing water through his spout, just floating on the swell as if everything else was too much bother, now and then closing his small eyes as if all he wanted to do was sleep.

Shoals of tuna and bonito and sardines—the whale's favourite—dashed past and crowded boisterously around the surface, but he pretended to ignore them and simply floated there like a log, although really he was rather too big for a log.

He was a sardine whale, so named for their snack of choice. Sardine whales average about sixteen metres long, but our whale floating here so terribly listlessly was uncommonly large at twenty metres, and weighed in at thirty tons—and to make matters worse, he was a male.

Unlike humans, female whales are bigger than males, and the bigger they are, the more splendid they are thought to be. And not just by the humans who hunt them for their meat and their oil, but by their very own fellow whales.

For the males, it wasn't so much a case of the smaller the better, but if like our whale they were bigger than the females, beyond what was acceptable, so to speak, then the females seemed to find them repulsive and refused to have anything to do with them.

Upon reaching adulthood, whales find a mate and travel the oceans together, giving birth to a baby whale once every two years. But this male was too big, and however hard he tried to attract a mate, emitting subsonic signals to alert the young females to a passing shoal of sardines or giving them gifts of shrimp, they simply ate their fill and then quickly swam away as if repelled at the mere sight of his enormous body.

In other words, our whale was a complete flop with the ladies. It wouldn't have been so bad if he'd just been bad-tempered or ugly—after all, there was some chance of finding a quirky female who was attracted to ill-natured males or odd looks. But being too big was a no-no. They were all scared of him.

He considered various possibilities, like maybe he ate too much and that was why he'd grown so big, or how he might join the larger finback whales in Antarctica—but when he tried to shrink himself by eating smaller quantities of shrimps and sardines he just got dizzy, and he couldn't bear the thought of living in such icy waters.

Whenever he happened to be near the pod he always felt anxious, so most of the time he stayed alone, eating and sleeping, then waking and spending the entire day rocked by the waves. At times it suddenly occurred to him that somewhere in the ocean there must be a female bigger than him, his perfect mate must be feeling lonesome waiting for him, and so he would rouse himself and swim off in a random direction.

Overhead a never-ending stream of aeroplanes flew northwards and then returned southwards, sometimes belching thin trails of smoke from their engines or flying so low and unsteadily that it seemed they would crash at any moment. These were the American bombers conducting air raids on the Japanese archipelago far to the north, although of course the whale didn't know this. There were also numerous ships, big and small, ploughing through the waves in a great hurry.

When the whale was little his mother had taught him that, if he ever saw a ship, he had to quickly dive into the depths and stay down as long as his breath lasted, swimming as far away from it as he could. Even if the ship was smaller than him, aboard there was an extremely cruel type of animal called a human. Upon catching sight of a whale, these humans immediately took it for an enemy and gave chase, firing harpoons at it. She herself had twice barely escaped with her life, and the horror of those memories still brought tears to her eyes as she told him about them.

"Had you done anything nasty to them?" he'd asked, unable to comprehend why the humans would hate whales that much. "Of course not! On the contrary, we are the most intelligent animals in the sea and quite capable of befriending humans," she replied, adding with a sigh, "If they were just a little kinder, we could even save them when they get into trouble."

This was true. Whales have the biggest brains of all animals, and are very intelligent. Long ago, dogs had become man's best friend by helping hunters, and whales could have done the same for humans at sea. But the humans just carried on killing them, and it was even said that whales would be extinct within twenty or thirty years unless they stopped.

Our whale, too, upon sighting a ship would hurriedly dive down and hold his breath, just as his mother had taught him, but there had been times when he wasn't paying attention and only noticed the ship when he was almost right by it. At such times he had closed his eyes tight waiting for the stab of the fearsome harpoon, but the humans had never shown him any violence, instead just calling, "Look at that whale—it's taking a nap!" as they sailed on by, waving at him.

"Maybe humans aren't such a terrible animal after all," he thought, and had once ventured to swim alongside a ship about the same size as himself. But then the humans had shouted, "Hey, don't come so close! If we're hit by something as big as you, we'll sink." Then there was the time he'd seen a single human inside a clumsy round, yellow boat that looked a bit like a sunfish. When that human, who appeared to have been injured, caught sight of the whale, he'd said, "You gonna tow me to America, my friend?"

The whale had come of age in the winter spanning 1944 to 1945, when the war between Japan and America was drawing ever closer to the Japanese mainland. The humans who'd waved at him were Japanese soldiers on their way to defend Iwo Jima against the Americans and, aware of their impending death, they'd been envious of the peacefully napping whale. The small ship he'd swum alongside was a fishing boat there to detect the American planes as they headed for Japan, while the man in the clumsy little yellow boat was an American pilot who'd been shot down and was hoping against hope that he might be rescued. Far from wanting to kill the whale, they knew they themselves might die at any time and so they were friendly towards him.

By around mid-August, although he was fairly far south, the whale began to feel the first signs of autumn, and now and then he was rocked by an unexpectedly large swell whipped up by the baby typhoons forming even farther to the south of where he was napping.

"There aren't any planes flying today, either," he thought to himself. The sky that had been so busy was now completely still. Aeroplanes and whales had really nothing in common, but he had enjoyed watching the flocks of planes high in the sky as they headed north trailing white smoke, and in his solitude had even called out to them. Sometimes they would catch the sunlight and glitter like his beloved sardines, and the low-flying planes were shaped just like seagulls.

At sundown, the whale entered a narrow inlet on a small island. Until three months ago humans had been here endlessly digging holes, but he hadn't seen them recently and he felt as if everyone was abandoning him. Day turned to night, and night to day, in endless repetition. If that was all there was to life, he thought only half in jest, then he might as well die! He started swimming towards a clump of rocks at the end of the inlet. It was dangerous to go so fast in the narrow space between sheer cliffs, but the hell with it.

When he was within a whisker of the rocks, he turned sharply and headed back out to sea at top speed. He was swimming as fast as he could when, in the sea under the cliff to one side of him, he caught sight of something he hadn't seen for a while. For the past year he'd just felt sad whenever he came across other whales in the pod, so whenever he heard them chatting he would swim off as fast as he could. But he hadn't forgotten them even for a moment. Wasn't that one of them—and a female at that—hiding away there?

And what was more, this female was bigger than he was, at least half as big again. Even the blue whale females that he'd heard about couldn't be as big as this one.

Surprised, the whale first passed right by her, then, feeling a little calmer, he closed each eye in turn, as if winking, to check whether or not he was dreaming. A human might pinch himself in similar circumstances, but this is what whales do.

Ever so gently, using just his tail to propel him along, the whale approached. From her colour and shape, she was indeed another sardine whale. If he was really honest, her dorsal fin was a little on the large side, but her colour was good and she was nicely chubby, and altogether she was a splendid specimen. Right now, though, she appeared to be asleep.

The whale swam slowly around her wondering how he could strike up a conversation. They would make the perfect couple, she and he! A normal male would be only half her size and they would look more like mother and child. But he was just right for her, he thought, gradually growing in confidence. Impatient for her to wake up, he nudged her with his body.

But this was not a female of his own species, it was a submarine of the Japanese naval fleet.

Iwo Jima and Okinawa had both been occupied, and only the Japanese mainland remained to be defended. As a last resort, Japan had made many small submarines that were to be crashed into enemy ships. At thirty metres long and weighing fifty tons they were more or less the size of a blue whale. And it was one of these that was hiding in the inlet.

Inside the submarine, the captain and chief engineer were in deep discussion. At midday that day, Japan's unconditional surrender had been broadcast on the radio.

"It must be misinformation by the enemy."

"All the same, it sounded pretty authentic."

"Even if it's true, we won't surrender. For the glory of the Imperial Navy, we will go ahead with the suicide attack against the enemy fleet as planned."

"But it's an imperial decree, so won't we be betraying the Emperor himself?"

"But simply raising the white flag means submitting to the enemy brutes!"

"Perhaps it would be more honourable to blow ourselves up?"

It was in the midst of their discussion that the whale had sidled up to them and bumped them in a display of his affection. Since the submarine depended on the correct balance between buoyancy and gravity to remain afloat, even just the slightest force made it sway alarmingly.

"Enemy attack! Prepare to counter depth charges!"

A depth charge was an explosive that was detonated in the sea to destroy submarines. Convinced that it was under attack, the submarine began to submerge.

Taken aback, the whale worried that he was being rejected yet again, and hurriedly began explaining for all he was worth: "Please don't run away! I didn't mean to wake you up. I don't want to hurt you, I just want to talk. I think you're gorgeous!" and dived down alongside the object of his affections, trying to snuggle up to her.

Now the submarine found itself being pushed upwards and pitched forwards. They should have heard depth charges exploding, but as it happened, everything was quiet. "We must have been caught up in an exceptionally strong current. Let's surface. Blow the main tank!" the captain ordered, although they were still upside down.

"What the heck?" As the upper half of the submarine floated above the surface of the ocean the captain leapt out onto the deck and was relieved to see no enemy in sight, but then he caught sight of something black nestling close to them in the moonlight.

He had no idea what it could be, but when it spouted water he realized it must be a whale. He and the chief engineer

stared at it. The whale, for his part, was astonished to see humans emerging from his beloved, but more importantly she didn't seem to dislike him and remained floating by his side. And so he floated there with her, entranced.

The next morning, he went out to sea and herded a shoal of sardines into the inlet so that she could have breakfast. She hadn't said a word all night, and hadn't moved an inch, so he worried that she might be ill and brought some nutritious seaweed for her too. Then he implored her to leave this small inlet and come out to the open sea where they could swim freely and feed on shoals of shrimp.

But the submarine had no intention of doing any such thing. Having discussed the matter, the crew had decided to fight against America until the bitter end, and were now feverishly making preparations, putting on fresh underwear and writing farewell notes to their loved ones. "How about tying our farewell notes to the tail of that weird whale?" suggested the chief engineer, thinking that one day someone would catch the whale and find the notes.

One of the crew members took the bundle wrapped in oilskin, dived into the sea, and tied it to the whale's tail. Thinking that the female had at last accepted his advances and was sending him a gift, the whale allowed the bundle to be attached to his tail, where it fluttered like a ribbon.

Two days later, the submarine set sail in search of the American fleet, with the whale following joyously in tow. If they could find somewhere with plenty of sardines and shrimps, he thought, they would be able to start a family.

"A child with the two of us for parents is going to be awesome. If it's a male, he's going to have to work hard to find himself a big enough female, but that's all right. I eventually managed to find myself a wonderful mate," he thought glancing over at her, only to find that she had planted herself on the seabed thirty metres down and was refusing to move.

"So you weren't feeling well after all. I'm so sorry I made you come along! Now you've gone and worn yourself out." Whales are mammals, not fish, and need to go to the surface to breathe, so if she stayed like that she would die. The whale tried hard to push her up to the surface, but it was no good.

Upon leaving the shelter of the island, the submarine had immediately appeared on the Americans' radar, and all their ships specialized in submarine attack had converged on the area under orders to sink any vessel that refused to surrender. When surrounded like this, the only thing to do was to cut the engines, speak in whispers and sit still as a rock. The submarine had taken water into the tanks for weight, and even the whale wouldn't be able to budge it so much as an inch.

The whale became frantic with worry and swam hysterically around his beloved, but the gathered ships mistook

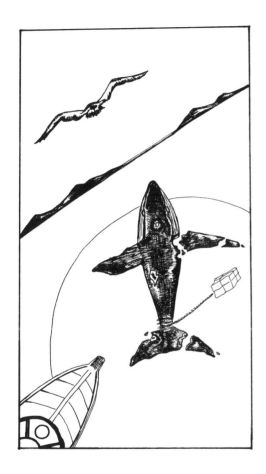

him for the submarine and threw out a depth charge. Shocked by the loud explosion he swam off, but they gave chase. If he had headed for the depths of the ocean bed he might have saved himself, but he was anxious for his new love. How awful having something so terrible thrown at you when you were unwell! It was so unlucky to have this happen just when he'd at last found himself a mate, he thought woefully. But he didn't want to be alone any more, so if she had to die then they would die together. After all, he would never chance upon such a wonderful mate as her again.

When the whale turned round and began swimming furiously towards the submarine's hiding spot, a depth charge exploded right above him. Half his body was blown off, but still he desperately tried to reach his beloved and it took another few depth charges to blow his huge, twenty-metre body to smithereens.

It was only three hours later that the ships dispersed, apparently satisfied. The submarine crew waited until they heard the propellers receding into the distance before nervously resurfacing.

The ocean was stained red. At first they thought it was the sunset, but then realized that actually it was the whale's blood. Looking closer, they could see bits of the whale's flesh, bones and tail strewn all over the waves. The American ships had mistaken the remains of the whale rising to the surface for fragments of the submarine.

The whale that had been making a nuisance of himself by hanging around them had saved their lives. Wordlessly, they saluted the sea of blood.

"Captain, look over there!" said one of the crew, pointing at the bundle of farewell notes, still tied like a ribbon to the whale's tail bobbing on the waves amidst the scraps of flesh. "Shall we go get it?"

"Leave it be," said the captain, shaking his head. After the whale had sacrificed itself for their sake, his previous fanaticism had entirely dissipated and he no longer wanted to engage in any more pointless killing.

The sunset faded, but the little submarine remained floating there in the red sea.

The Parrot
and the Boy

The 15th of August 1945

In the foothills of the mountains, some distance from the town, a boy and his parrot were living in a small air-raid shelter. The boy had just turned eight years old, but the age of his parrot, which the boy's sailor father had brought back from a southern isle as a gift for him, was unknown.

The parrot had a yellow crown-like crest and a touch of red at the base of its wings, as if bleeding, but otherwise it was covered all over with soft blue feathers. From its ugly, wrinkled feet you might think it was quite old, but then the mischievous look in its eye was altogether childlike, and at any rate parrots were said to live for a hundred years so there was no way of knowing. But the boy, who was an only child, had decided that it was his little sister.

21

For the past couple of weeks, the boy and the parrot had been hiding day and night in the darkness of the shelter.

An air-raid shelter was a place to keep you safe from the attacks by enemy planes, and they had been built in all major cities all over Japan from around 1942. Big shelters were tunnelled into the hillside and reinforced with wood or concrete, and could accommodate tens or even hundreds of people. There were also little shelters known as "octopus pots", which were just about the size of the holes people dug to dispose of household waste, and were meant for one person to quickly jump inside to escape machine-gun fire.

At that time, not so long ago, American planes were flying day and night over all of Japan's main cities, and people spent more time hunched up in air-raid shelters than they did in their own homes. The shelter the boy and his parrot were in was a pit 1 metre wide, 1.3 metres deep and 7 metres long, covered by planks of wood with half a metre of earth piled on top.

Originally it had been constructed at the side of the road, but in the air raid two months earlier the town had been completely razed to the ground all the way from the mountain to the sea, and in the burnt-out ruins it was no longer possible to tell where houses had once stood and roads had once run. The shelter was surrounded by piles of scorched roof tiles, sheets of corrugated iron, blackened telegraph poles and bits

of plasterboard. Nobody would even notice it was there unless they were looking for it.

The sizzling midsummer sun beat down on the ruins of the town, but inside the shelter was dark, and it was damp from the water that poured in whenever it rained. The boy was sitting on one of two wooden pallets on the floor, and the parrot's cage was on the other. The boy was so hungry that he barely had the energy to move, but the parrot would now and then playfully hang upside down, or screech loudly *Konnichi wa!* (Hello!)

In truth, though, the parrot wasn't being playful. Rather, it was worried that the boy hadn't said anything for some time. It even tried singing his favourite song: *Seagulls are / good sailors*

/ Regimented / good sailors / Their white hats, their white shirts, everything in white / They... Here it got stuck. Before, the boy would have looked a little exasperated and, tapping in time on its cage, finished the last line for it: "They float splashing / on the waves. Try it again!"

Whyareyoulookingsoglum?DidMamagiveyouascolding? The parrot tried hard to talk to the boy, but after all it was just a bird. It could imitate human speech, but whenever it spoke its own language it just sounded like screeching to humans.

The boy heard the parrot, but merely glanced at it before sinking back into his own thoughts. Before he would have worried that maybe it was being attacked by a cat, or had run out of food, and would have tickled its yellow crown with his finger, or stroked its wrinkled feet.

The boy had really doted on the parrot. When his father had brought it home with him his mother had said irritably, "There's not enough food even for us people these days. A bird that lays eggs might be useful, but a *parrot*?" His father was away at sea and hardly ever home, and his mother was busy with the neighbourhood watch group, doing the shopping, gathering firewood and all the air-raid drills, so it was hardly surprising that she wasn't exactly overjoyed at having to take on a useless parrot on top of everything else.

The boy, though, had immediately taken to the brightly coloured tropical bird. He loved the mischievous look in its eyes, and was astonished when it repeated *You okay?* in exactly the same tone of voice as his father. Apparently, during the long voyage back to Japan, the parrot had looked so unwell that his father had asked it so many times, "You okay?" that it had memorized the phrase.

The boy promised solemnly that he would take care of the parrot, feed it and clean out its cage, and so he was allowed to keep it. In 1942, it was still possible to get hold of bird feed such as sunflower seeds and hempseed. Few people were keeping birds at that time, and while such things were in short supply, they weren't much use to people and the bird shops had leftover stocks.

The boy didn't know if the parrot was male or female but, having decided it was like a little sister to him, he named it Setchan. When his mother was out, he would sit before the parrot and talk to it, teaching it songs and various words.

The parrot didn't know it, but in the spring of 1942 the boy's father lost his life when his ship was sunk by an American warplane near the Philippines. The boy's mother had insisted, "He died for our country so you mustn't cry," but when the parrot called out *You okay?* in his father's voice, he simply couldn't hold back the tears.

And though his mother now no longer disapproved of him keeping the parrot, it was increasingly difficult to get hold of bird feed. Once the bird shops' stocks ran out, the boy fed it on wheat, rice and even the flour they used to make noodles, though it meant that he had less to eat himself. His mother began growing cucumbers, tomatoes, aubergines and other vegetables in their small garden to supplement the meagre rations, and at the edge of the plot she planted a few sunflowers for the parrot. After all, it was a keepsake of her late husband.

When summer came, enormous blooms twenty centimetres across not only provided food for the yellow-crested parrot, but looked so gorgeous that she planted more in the autumn. All the neighbours mocked her for wasting good land on a bird but, come New Year, they were shocked when everyone was ordered to grow sunflowers in their gardens. Of course this wasn't to provide food for the parrot; the seeds were pressed to make oil to be used in the war effort. The countries they had occupied in the south were oil-rich, but the ships transporting their produce to Japan were all sunk en route. It wasn't long before urgent orders were issued to extract oil and alcohol from pine roots and potatoes as well as sunflowers.

Sunflowers were planted all along the narrow streets and on open land on the mountainside behind. Each household had a quota. The boy and his mother had already planted them the year before, so things went smoothly and they had a bumper harvest. However, their plot of land was quite small, and when they took out what they needed for the parrot's food, there just wasn't enough left to meet their quota.

Their neighbours, however, were unsympathetic. "This is no time to be growing food for a pet bird," they said. "Besides, parrots are American brutes too, aren't they? Kill it!" The boy tried to explain that it was a memento of his dead father, but they wouldn't listen and took most of the seeds away, leaving only a pitiful few for the parrot.

His mother accepted that this was only to be expected during wartime, but the boy couldn't bear to see the parrot looking so dejected at the lack of food. That night he slipped out of the house and found a plot some distance away where the sunflowers hadn't yet been harvested and stole some seeds. He stored these, and more from subsequent night-time sorties, under the veranda.

Every now and then they were discovered and he received a thorough telling-off, but it didn't occur to anybody that he was feeding them to the parrot, so he escaped any more severe punishment.

Eventually the air raids started for real and they were forced to run for the shelter whenever the warning sounded. The parrot's cage was over half the boy's own height, but he would always take it with him. The parrot of course understood nothing about the seeds or the air raids, and perhaps thought the boy was playing with him for it frolicked merrily in the shelter. While the grown-ups cowered in anticipation of the fearsome sound of the enemy bombs, it would screech at the top of its voice *You okay?* and sing *Seagulls are good sailors*

27

hopelessly out of tune. The grown-ups naturally were annoyed, and grumbled, "The air-raid shelters are for people, not birds. Get rid of the disgusting thing!" so after that he had to leave the parrot behind at home.

And then, six months ago, his neighbourhood was targeted by the B-29s. The sound of the incendiary bombs and explosions was terrifying. However hard he blocked up his ears, it felt as though the noise was seeping in through each and every one of his pores. He clung to his mother, but after some time the grown-ups decided that if they stayed in the shelter they would likely burn to death, so they decided to evacuate. The boy's mother too dragged him by the hand towards the mountain.

But he couldn't leave the parrot behind! He told his mother to wait a moment, and bravely set off as fast as his legs would carry him through all the whistles and whooshes of the falling incendiary bombs. He had just grabbed the parrot's cage and was crawling under the veranda to retrieve some of the sunflower seeds he'd squirrelled away there when suddenly there was a bright flash and a roar in his ears. For a moment he couldn't see or hear anything, just he could smell burning. "Mama! *Mama!*" he screamed, struggling to his feet. The next thing he knew he was standing on the corner of a street he didn't recognize, still clutching the parrot's cage and bag of sunflower seeds.

Of course he didn't recognize it,

for all the 250kg bombs had blown the entire neighbourhood to smithereens, and his mother and those cantankerous neighbourhood watch members along with it.

The boy did as his mother had always told him, and went into the air-raid shelter to wait for her there. With nobody left to extinguish the fires, the remains of the houses continued burning for some time. Once the flames had died down, some officials came around to check the damage. Noting all the bomb craters, they shook their heads and muttered, "Awful. Just awful," and went away again. They didn't notice the boy and his parrot hiding in the shelter.

The boy stopped talking altogether. Or rather, he couldn't talk. The shock had been so immense that he had completely forgotten how. However hard he tried to call out "Mama!" his voice seemed to stick in the back of his throat and the only sounds that came out were "Mmn unhhh." He couldn't even remember the word he used to call his sweet mother, who had always been there at his bedside darning clothes in the dim light whenever he awoke at night.

Of course he was hungry, and at night when nobody was around he would slip into the burnt remains of vegetable plots to steal cucumbers and aubergines, and gnaw on potato leaves. For the time being he had enough food for the parrot which, now that it was just the two of them, would babble away cheerfully, *Hello... You okay?... Oh dear... Hahahahaha!*

But in fact the parrot was beside itself with worry for the boy, who never spoke to it any more. *Whydon'tyoutalktomeanymore?WheredidMamago?*

In the darkness of the shelter, where night and day didn't exist, the boy gradually became thinner and thinner. Sometimes he would do his best to rouse himself and try to speak, straining his whole body to produce a sound, but it never came out as words.

Whenever the parrot uttered its best phrase, *You okay?*, his eyes would light up. Since he had lost his power of speech, he hadn't been able to understand what the parrot said either, but even so the words made him feel terribly nostalgic and he tried desperately to copy the sounds: *Yu… yuuo.*

The parrot was happy finally to get a reaction from the boy, and repeated over and over again, *You okay? You okay?* in exactly the same tone as the boy's father had used. The boy was silent for a while, but eventually he managed to thickly articulate the sounds *You okay?*

The parrot was delighted and screeched in his own language, *Waaah!That'smyboy!* It didn't know the boy was in shock from the bomb blast, and had been fretting all this time that he was angry with it. It started babbling happily, *Hello… Oh dear oh dear!* This is what the boy's mother had always said. *Don't do that!… No!* The boy mumbled each phrase after him, and as he began speaking the words, little by little as if in a dream, the reality of the air raid began to sink in.

31

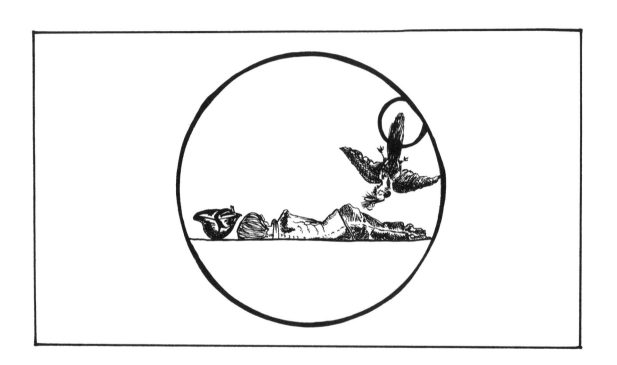

Mama's dead. Those bombs… The moment this thought came to him, his strength drained from him, but he quickly said, "No, she isn't dead. As long as I wait here, she'll come looking for me. Won't she, Setchan?" Hearing its name, the parrot screeched *Setchan!* and launched into *Seagulls are good sailors*. The boy too was drawn in and began singing along, but he couldn't form the words as well as the parrot. When he got stuck on *They float splashing / on the waves*, the parrot laughed merrily, *Ha ha ha ha!*, just as the boy used to do.

On 15th August, the war between Japan and America ended. Some of the people living in the burnt-out ruins were angry, some were tearful and some heaved a deep sigh of relief, but in the small air-raid shelter at the foot of the mountain, some distance from the town, the boy was trying his hardest to relearn words from the parrot.

Just as the parrot had once learnt from the boy, now it patiently repeated the same words over again, and the boy repeated them, savouring each one. But by the time the boy finally was able to speak again, he was too hungry to stand.

The parrot frantically screeched at the once again silent boy, *You okay? You okay?* The boy's faint *okay…* was the last word he spoke. And three days after the boy died, the parrot that was supposed to live a hundred years ran out of food and toppled from its perch, never to move again.

The Mother That Turned into a Kite

The 15th of August 1945

The summer sun beat down on the burnt-out ruins that stretched uninterrupted from the mountains all the way to the sea. At a glance the ruins looked like nothing more than a reddish-brown wasteland, but in fact they were more than just rubble.

The blackened remnants of telegraph poles and toilet bowls, cash boxes, water pipes, bed frames, sewing-machine bobbin cases, wire-reinforced glass and various other bits of wreckage half buried in the ground were testament to the daily lives of the people who had until recently been living here.

Crouching amidst all this debris was a child. He was five years old, but his face was as shrivelled as an old man's and utterly lacking in any signs of life.

Hungry or starving children everywhere all look the same, whether in Biafra or refugees from Vietnam, or, to go back a bit further in time, in the coal mines of Kyushu, or, still further back, the street urchins you would find outside any station in Japan's major cities. They all have a face like an upside-down triangle with enormous eyes, wide open but unseeing, the pupils unmoving, and a mouth puckered as though the skin from their face has been tucked into it.

This child's name was Katchan. Ever since the town had burnt down, Katchan had remained crouching here looking up at the sky. That summer, 1945, had seen the endlessly clear skies criss-crossed constantly by aeroplanes, but Katchan didn't even notice them. He was waiting for his mother, who was sure to come back from the sky—the mother who had soared up into the sky like a kite blown by the wind.

Ten days before, the town in which Katchan and his mother lived had been the target of an air raid. It was a residential neighbourhood with no factories or military installations whatsoever, but the unpredictable B-29s dropped their incendiary bombs on it anyway, starting fires that spread rapidly. Some people evacuated immediately and managed to reach the safety of the elementary school grounds, but Katchan's mother had dilly-dallied.

She was convinced that his father, called up two years earlier, would come

home safe and sound from the front, and when he did so he would need something to wear other than his uniform. Therefore, without bothering about her own kimonos, she put together a set of clothing for him along with his beloved fishing tackle, and was just dithering over his books when their house was filled with ominous black smoke from the spreading fires.

She grabbed Katchan's hand, hoisted the bundle onto her back and rushed out into the street. They headed for the elementary school, but their path was blocked by a sea of flames, while from the opposite direction came the cracking and popping of the flames engulfing roofs that were eerily lit up by the blaze.

"Hold onto my hand tight," she shouted at Katchan, and set off at a trot in the direction where the flames seemed less intense. Incendiary bombs were still falling all around, and she couldn't tell whether she was headed east or west. She stopped briefly to dunk their air-raid hoods in some water, before continuing along the darkest possible streets like a thief. Everyone must have fled already, for they didn't come across a single person.

They ran past fire-fighting hoses lying like snakes on the road, upturned buckets strewn around and the body of a man who had been hit by a bomb. She clasped Katchan tightly to her and he struggled to breathe, but he knew very well that now was not the time to whine.

Suddenly she dropped him on the

ground with a thud. He thought they'd run quite some way, but now, looking around, he saw they were in the little park not far from their house. It had a small playground, with just a sandpit and a swing, and Katchan knew it well. They were now surrounded by a solid wall of flames and unable to escape any farther.

His mother breathed heavily for a while, then drew Katchan into her arms and crouched down low as she checked around her. She had jumped into what had been a sandpit, although a couple of years earlier all the sand had been taken out and distributed around the neighbourhood to use for extinguishing fires. It was kept in pots known as "fire-fighting grenades" that were displayed in department store windows.

The sound of the blaze grew fiercer. The houses surrounding the park had not yet caught fire, but it was clearly just a matter of time. Even now the flames were so strong that the fire didn't simply spread from house to house but rather caused each house to explode. As the air grew hotter and hotter they began to feel as though they were breathing fire, and even all the leaves on the trees seemed to tremble and scream in the heat.

If it was already like this now, what would it be like when the fire came even closer? Katchan's mother glanced around in search of water, but there was none. If only there was some sand left in the pit they would be able to burrow down into it to bear the heat a little better, but the hardened earth base was all that was there.

He heard a hissing sound of escaping vapour, and saw something that looked more like steam than smoke spewing from under the eaves and out of the windows of a two-storey house. He'd never seen anything like it before, and it really felt as though the house was in its death throes. A sharp snap was accompanied by a flurry of sparks. It was like being in a nightmare, but now was no time for watching in fascination. There was no breeze and the smoke was rising straight up into the sky rather than blowing into the park, but even so his eyes were stinging. His mother covered his body with hers and told him, "Katchan, close your eyes tight. Don't worry, everything will be fine."

Whoosh, snap, whoosh, snap. Now he felt as though his throat was on fire, and his air-raid hood was bone dry. *If only there was some water!* As his mother raised her head to look around again, refusing to give up, a fresh blast of hot air stung his head.

Even with their eyes tightly shut they could still clearly see the colour of the blaze. For the first time his mother was afraid. "Papa!" she called out to her husband on the front line. Hearing this, Katchan also felt that for the sake of his father they couldn't die here. There must be some way to survive!

Their faces were parched, but under their clothes they were sweating uncomfortably. Suddenly his mother had an idea: she stuck her hand down the front of her clothes, scooped up some sweat, and rubbed it over Katchan's face as if it were lotion.

"Hang on in there Katchan, we can do it!"

Even her sweat was hot, she thought, as she desperately fumbled for more. If only the trickle of perspiration could be more like a waterfall. When she rubbed it on Katchan's bare hands and feet, the dryness gave way to a smooth and pleasant sensation, as if he'd just got out of the bath.

As she busied herself protecting Katchan with her sweat, she managed to forget her fear. But the fire was burning as fiercely as ever, roaring and popping, sending telegraph poles up like burning torches and shrivelling the leaves on the trees in the park. But eventually her sweat dried up. Her mouth was dry too. There was no more moisture left.

"Mama!" cried Katchan. As long as he was with his mother, he believed that he would be okay whatever happened. But still, he needed to call her now and then to make sure she hadn't left him.

When she heard him call, she didn't feel frightened so much as sad. Three years ago, when it still seemed as though Japan would win the war, she and Katchan would come to this park and bask in the sun. While she unpicked an old sweater to knit into warm socks for his father, Katchan would totter around or play in the sandpit making mountains and valleys with his little spade. On Sundays Papa would come with them and they'd take pictures of them together.

Whoever could have imagined them being surrounded by flames like this in the very same park, the very same sandpit? She could hear little Katchan's voice as he romped around, and then she could see his laughing face, and before she knew it the hands she was holding over her face were wet with tears.

Unthinkingly she rubbed her wet hands over Katchan's hot face. Only then did she realize they were her tears. For a while they kept coming, but as she became absorbed in the task of moistening Katchan's parched skin, her sadness faded and they dried up.

She tried hard to think of sad things, like how grief-stricken Papa would be to learn the son he had doted on was dead. She had seen many charred bodies of children killed in air raids, and how awful it was to think that cute little Katchan might end up dying the same way without ever having tasted any delicious food, or played with toys or visited any amusement parks.

She didn't know which illnesses caused the most suffering, but surely there was nothing so painful as being slowly roasted to death. Whatever had Katchan done to deserve this? She conjured up the most desolate thoughts possible to make herself sadder and sadder, and every time her tears came welling up she rubbed them onto Katchan's skin.

Then she started singing him a lullaby, making up the words as she went.

Time for bed, little Katsuhiko
Close your eyes and in your world
Nothing will scare you any more
Time to sleep, little Katsuhiko
No need to be scared any more
You're only five after all...

If he had to die, surely it was better he did so in his sleep. But her voice was hoarse from her dry throat and was drowned out by the popping of the fire, so Katchan never heard it.

If you have to die, don't suffer too much
If you have to die, let it be in your sleep
If you have to die, let it be while you dream
And give all your suffering to me
If you have to die, then go to sleep
If you have to die, I'll sing you a lullaby

At last her tears ran dry. She could no longer see anything for the smoke in her eyes, but she wanted somehow or other to be able to moisten Katchan's skin. She scratched at the earth, but it was bone-dry. She bared her breast to protect Katchan's skin with her own. He had been a clingy baby and had breastfed up until last year, so when she did so he instinctively fumbled for her nipple and tried suckling her milk. Surely the milk wouldn't come, but even so she desperately tried to relive those moments when he'd been a baby. How could she ever forget those important memories!

But the fire was getting closer and closer, and now three sides were ablaze, and the park's trees appeared to bloom with sparks, and in her confusion the memories only came in fragments: Katchan, still in her belly, stretching his legs out as if in pleasure when she got into the bath; surprising her by moving around inside her in the middle of the night. *Here you go, your little soldier*, the midwife had remarked, holding him up for her to see, and she had laughed because he looked so much like his Papa, and he'd sucked on her nipples so fiercely, squirming and groping for her other nipple with his hand, but ending up clutching at the smooth mattress instead. When at first her milk hadn't come, she'd resorted to massaging her breast and had been shocked as it spurted out as high as the ceiling, and when it was time to wean him she'd been told to spread mustard on her nipple, but she hadn't been able to bring herself to do that to him.

She desperately kneaded her breast and, cradling Katchan like an unweaned baby, gave it to him to suckle on. If just a little came out, then he could drink it, or she could use it to moisten his skin as she'd done with her sweat and tears. *Mother horse and her sweet foal, always happy together, clippety clop clippety clop, peacefully walking along...* when Katchan was just beginning to talk, he'd loved this song and squealed in delight when it came to *clippety clop clippety clop*. That big rattle and musical box and summer kimono Papa had bought for him had been such rare treasures, and even nappies had been hard to come by, and the terrible fits that Katchan had suffered… memories of him as a baby came flooding back to her. But she had reached the limit of her strength. Now she wasn't surrounded by flames, but together with Papa gazing at Katchan's smooth baby face as he slept.

She no longer felt the heat, and suddenly she noticed that Katchan was greedily sucking in his cheeks drinking her milk. "Wait a moment, there'll be more," she said, regaining her senses again. Removing her nipple from Katchan's mouth she squeezed with both hands and rubbed the trickle of milk over his face, hands, legs, chest and tummy. This would be better than drinking it now, and would make things more bearable for him. The trickle soon stopped, so she rubbed her nipples directly onto his body until all the milk dried up.

Now she was beginning to get light-headed in the glare of heat. She tried to focus, but was at a loss as to what else she could do. Katchan and Papa began to recede into the distance and she felt an overwhelming desire to sleep. The raging blaze and collapsing houses seemed to belong to another world.

"Mama, I'm hot!" Katchan clung to his exhausted mother and screamed, "Mama, I'm scared!" Hearing his cries, his mother came to again and thought— *water. Anything wet! I have to find some for Katchan.*

But what could she do? Her own body was so dry that it could burn like a matchstick at any moment. She held

Katchan tightly to her and focused all her mind on that one word, *water. Water!* She no longer even really knew what it was, *waterwaterwater*, only that it could save Katchan, *waterwaterwater*. She chanted it over and over like a spell, and as she did so blood began seeping from her pores and dripped over Katchan in her arms, *waterwaterwater*, even as she was losing consciousness she prayed harder and her blood began pouring out, covering Katchan from head to foot.

Eventually the flames died down and the hot air was sucked up into the sky, the smoke dispersed by the breeze, and blue sky appeared. "Mama!" called Katchan, becoming aware of his surroundings again. He shook his mother, who was still covering him with her body, but she slipped to the ground, flat and dry, with no moisture left in her at all.

His mother's body floated up in the strong breeze that always followed an air raid. "Mama, where are you going?" Katchan called in surprise, but his mother merely smiled at him the same way she always did. Relieved, he ran after her, but then a strong gust of wind suddenly whipped her up and away, higher and higher into the sky. "Mama!" he called again and again, and each time she turned to look back at him. Like a kite her body was drawn up into the post-blaze sky, and remained dancing there like an angel until eventually she disappeared from view.

Katchan waited. His mother would definitely come back. He was hungry and thirsty, but he crouched, waiting for her, not moving from the spot where he'd seen her soaring up into the sky like a kite. He didn't feel particularly lonely, as he felt she was up there in the sky watching over him, and also because she'd told him that his father's departing words as he left for the front had been, "He's a strong boy, you mark my words."

On 15th August, a little before the imperial message announcing the end of the war was broadcast over the ruins, Katchan's emaciated body too was blown away by the wind up into the sky. His mother had come to meet him, and they fluttered and danced together like two kites under the brilliant summer sun as they went up, up into the sky, looking down on the burnt-out ruins far below.

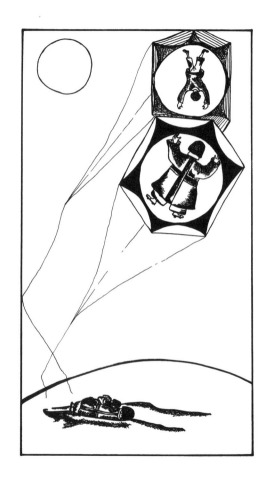

The Old She-Wolf
and the Little Girl

In Manchuria, now north-east China, a large she-wolf and a girl just four years old squatted in a sorghum field.

The wolf was sturdily built, but she was old and patches of her fur had fallen out and most of her teeth were missing. The little girl wore a white shirt with red baggy pantaloons, and was holding tightly onto a basket. They had been hiding here for two full days, as the earth rumbled from the countless large tanks heading south, and exchanges of gunfire sounded all around. Long ago, the old wolf had fled from humans with guns, and she had never forgotten the smell of gunpowder smoke.

The wolf was well aware that the time of her own death was approaching. Her eyes, which had once seen far into the distance even at night, were now blurred as if covered by a perpetual mist, and her ears, which had been able to distinguish between people's voices in the village in the next valley, were now quite deaf, so all she had to rely on was her sense of smell.

Until two years earlier she had reigned as leader of the pack of fifty-two cubs that she herself had given birth to and raised, but as she began to feel her age she had ceded to a younger wolf, and once she knew the end was not far off she had quietly set out in search of a place to die.

When she had been with the pack, she hadn't needed to hunt for food since the younger wolves would all offer her the choicest meat out of respect, and they had also taken turns to keep guard night and day, so there was no need for her to stay attuned to every noise.

Now she was on her own, however, she had to take care of everything herself. And with her nerves constantly on edge, her physical strength rapidly deteriorated. Although she was old, however, she did have her pride. It would be better to lie down on the railroad tracks that crossed the plain from north to south and be run over by a train than succumb to wild dogs or cats, she thought. And so she had once more drawn herself up and strained her useless eyes and ears to the utmost, hoping quickly to find a quiet place where she wouldn't be disturbed by birds or worms.

With this one wish in mind, she had continued walking unsteadily on and on. But about ten days ago a great commotion had broken out around her, the Japanese began moving southwards en masse, and aeroplanes with markings she hadn't seen before began flying around overhead.

The wolf only wanted to find a place to die as soon as possible and was not particularly startled by this. Nevertheless, the ruckus only grew daily and the sounds of human voices became ever more deafening, so she was no longer able to go peacefully on her way and was instead forced to hide in the woods by day and wait until nightfall to continue.

At dusk on the fifth day, as the wolf came out of the woods she ran into a large group of Japanese people rushing by in a panic. The wolf cursed her own carelessness, shrinking back at the thought of being targeted by their guns, but they didn't seem at all concerned with her as they called out to each other in shrill voices and, ignoring the wails of the children among them, hastened on their way.

The wolf had always warned the younger members of the pack that groups of Japanese were generally soldiers, most of whom were good marksmen, so they should never go near them, but this group seemed a bit different. They didn't smell of leather or look in the slightest menacing. In fact, most of them appeared to be women and children.

Instinctively the wolf followed them. She might be on the verge of death,

but she was still hungry. And there was nothing tastier than a human child, she thought, recalling how as a young wolf she had led her own cubs raiding human settlements. She followed stealthily after the group thinking that she would follow their scent for as long as it took. Even if they noticed her it wouldn't matter, for sooner or later they would tire and squat down for a rest, and that would be her opportunity.

But the humans just carried on and on, and showed no signs of stopping even when she thought it was about time they should be getting tired. And she herself was exhausted. However, she was determined that this should be her last hunt, so however unsteady she felt, she doggedly followed after them. And

just before dawn they came abruptly to a halt, a hush fell over them, and they lay down flat on the ground as if in fear of something.

Not far away was a Manchu village. The humans consulted amongst themselves, and then an old man stood up and went towards the village. As it grew light and the group became visible, the old wolf could see that, as she had thought, most of them were women and children, accompanied only by a few old men. All carried backpacks and water bottles, and had evidently been walking a long time for they all looked completely worn out, and now and then a child could be heard sobbing.

Finally the old man returned accompanied by three Manchu. She didn't know what they were talking about, but the Japanese crowded around them, their heads bowed in supplication. Just ten days earlier, this would have been unthinkable of the haughty Japanese. They had always yelled at Manchu, Koreans and White Russians as if they owned the place!

It seemed they were exchanging goods for food, and after a long discussion the group again dragged themselves on their way, their bodies heavy after the short rest. Even the voices of the mothers scolding their grizzling children sounded pitiful, as though they themselves were wailing.

Thirsty, the wolf took a drink from a small stream, then caught two field mice to appease her hunger. She had just started running as hard as she could to catch up with the group again when she suddenly caught sight of something red in the grass. Pricking up her ears, she could hear a hoarse voice crying. It didn't immediately occur to her that it might be a human child, but as she cautiously approached she saw a small girl tottering through the grass.

The only reason she didn't pounce on the girl and gobble her up right away was that the edge had been taken off her hunger by those two field mice. And then she was quite taken aback when the little girl showed absolutely no fear upon seeing her, but instead called out "Belle!" and flung her arms happily around her neck.

The girl stroked the wolf's neck and back, sobbing, "Where's Mama, Belle? Go find her for me!" The wolf didn't understand what she was saying, but the girl clearly thought that she was a friend and so she submitted to her, thinking how odd it was for a human to be so unafraid of a wolf.

The little girl didn't smell of the things the wolf hated most, leather and gunpowder, but instead was permeated with the scent of milk. This brought back memories of all the cubs that, not so long ago, she herself had given birth to and raised. Come to think of it, the little girl's sobbing voice was not unlike the wheedling cries of a newborn wolf cub.

Before the wolf realized what she was doing, she was cradling the little girl between her front paws, just as she had done with her own cubs, and was licking her face and hands, which still smelt of her mother's milk. The little girl snuggled up to her. Now and then she called loudly, "Mama!", but her only answer was the sound of the wind crossing the wide open plain. She began sobbing again, but when the wolf licked away her tears she became ticklish and wriggled.

When the wolf drank water, the little girl copied her, getting down on her hands and knees and drinking noisily. Then, feeling hungry, she took out some stale bread from her basket to munch on, first picking out the little sugar candy balls in it to give to the wolf. Sugar candy was not at all what the wolf was used to, but she tried licking it and, finding it quite tasty, rolled it around in her toothless mouth. She even began to feel renewed strength welling up in her flagging body.

"Belle, where do you think Mama went?" the little girl asked, and the wolf tilted her head inquisitively. It was the first time she'd ever heard of humans leaving a little girl alone in such a wilderness.

The little girl's name was Kiku. Kiku had been born in a big city in the north, where her father had been the director of a photographic studio. Japanese working in Manchuria often used to send photographs to their families back home, and soldiers too came to be photographed, so the business thrived and Kiku, her two elder brothers and

their German Shepherd Belle wanted for nothing. But in January that year the call-up papers arrived for her father, even though he was already in his forties, and in no time at all he was enlisted.

Their town, which had been relatively quiet even while the war was on, suddenly saw massive movements of troops. With Japan's defences in the south under increasing pressure, the Kwantung Army, which prided itself on being Japan's military elite, were being brought in as reinforcements. Kiku's mother and her family didn't know this, however. They all still believed that the northern defences were impenetrable, even if the Soviets had revoked the Soviet-Japanese Neutrality Pact.

By the time the Soviet forces attacked in overwhelming numbers on 6th August, the Kwantung Army was a mere shadow of its former self and made up only of older, raw recruits like Kiku's father, while their artillery and tanks had all been sent to defend Okinawa. The Japanese population quickly evacuated and fled southwards in what amounted to a stampede. The only option left to them was to travel overland, hoping that if they could just manage to reach Korea they would be saved.

The families of the military elite and the top executives of major Japanese firms in Manchuria had shrewdly assessed the situation before the Soviet invasion and had already left in a specially chartered train. The ordinary citizens had been left behind with no guarantees, and fled with just the clothes on their backs and whatever food they could carry, although at least to begin with they were able to take trains.

Kiku boarded a freight train with her mother and brothers in high spirits, having forgotten in all the excitement that they had come without Belle. She could feel the movement of the train through the rush matting, and she and her brothers imitated its clickety-clack until hushed by the grown-ups, who all seemed on edge. Now and then the train stopped, before slowly setting off again. They could hear the sound of explosions in the distance, and eventually Kiku too felt the heavy atmosphere in the carriage.

They were only given a little water to drink now and then, since they couldn't go outside to pee, and nobody knew when they would next be able to get hold of more supplies. Seated on the hard floor, leaning against her mother's knees, Kiku's bottom hurt. But at least they were on the train.

As they pulled into one station, they heard soldiers shouting, "All off the train! This train is stopping here." There was nothing for it but to obey the order and continue their journey on foot, with only the train tracks to guide them southwards to Korea. The group of women and children now set off at a snail's pace along the same route that until not so long ago the Asia Express had travelled at a speed of 120 kph.

Their journey was tougher than they had ever imagined possible. Being so weak they would easily fall prey to bandits, and the Manchu seemed to know that Japan had lost for they no longer felt the need to show them any kindness. They had to give up their wristwatches in exchange for water, and when they pleaded to be allowed to spend the night in a storage shed, they were flatly refused.

They cooked by night to avoid any smoke being spotted by the enemy during the day, and drew their drinking water from a stream. Eventually some of them started falling ill. As long as they could walk, everybody rallied together, but if they collapsed then nobody had the strength to help them up again. Whenever they sensed that bandits were around they all held their breath, and if a baby started crying at that moment they had to cover its mouth to silence it, even at the risk of smothering it.

Then, by a stroke of bad luck, Kiku came down with measles. Her mother noticed she had a fever but there were no medicines, and so she hoisted her onto her back and carried on walking. When red spots began appearing on her white skin, however, her mother knew it was hopeless. After all, there were so many small children in the group, and Kiku might give it to all of them. Her mother did her best to conceal them, but their elderly leader grew concerned about how listless Kiku had become, and the moment he saw her red spots he took her mother to one side.

She already knew what he was going to say. "It's awful, but we'll just have to leave her behind. She's not going to get better, anyway. If you really want to stay with her, then I'm afraid I will have to ask you to leave the group," he told her, his face expressionless. It was the obvious thing to do.

If she took her three children and left the group, the entire family would probably perish. She considered having her two sons continue with the group while she stayed behind with Kiku, but they were only eight and six years old and still needed their mother too. She wept bitterly, but eventually decided that she would just have to abandon Kiku, who was now delirious with fever. That was the only way. She breastfed her and filled a basket with stale bread, then waited for the next rest stop to furtively place her, fast asleep, in the long grass.

She prayed that she might be taken in by some compassionate being; perhaps someone from a nearby Manchu village would hear her crying. Doing her best to convince herself of this, she returned to the group and, holding her two sons by the hand, resumed the trek southwards. When the elder boy asked, "Where's Kiku?" she told him, "A kind old lady is looking after her because she's so cute."

When Kiku woke up she was taken aback to find herself all alone. Nevertheless, she felt reassured to see Belle, whom she'd thought they had left behind, at her side looking puzzled. As long as she was with Belle, she would definitely be able to find her way home—after all, Belle often used to disappear off somewhere and they would all worry about her, but she always came home.

That night the wolf held Kiku close to her until she fell asleep, and the next day she put her on her back and set off northwards at a trot. To begin with she felt she'd been saddled with an annoying burden, and didn't know what to do. At this rate, she'd never find a place where she could die in peace. But the child seemed unwell and was completely dependent on her, and she couldn't bring herself to abandon her.

Maybe it was the effect of the sugar candy Kiku had given her, but

she decided to summon the energy to return to the pack. The lively young pack members would all take turns to bring food and look after them, and in their care even this sickly child was bound to grow strong. With the renewed faith of a mother wolf, she forced her shaky legs onward step by step, and at length came to the battlefield where the volunteer corps were desperately putting up a resistance against the Soviet forces in the hope of gaining a little more time for their families fleeing southwards.

At last quiet reigned once more. The 15th of August in Manchuria was a cloudless day with clear blue skies.

They left the sorghum field to find Japanese corpses scattered everywhere. They had just one more mountain to cross before they would reach the valley where the wolf's pack lived. Even as the old wolf resented the curious turn of events that had disrupted her search for a peaceful place to die, ever since she had decided to take Kiku to the pack in the hope they would look after her, she had begun to lament keenly the fact of her own old age. But how heartless those humans were! Her own pack would never abandon a cub, whatever the circumstances.

Eventually Kiku's fever grew worse and she couldn't hold onto the wolf's back any longer. The wolf sank her few remaining teeth into the baggy trousers covering her limp body, braced her neck to avoid dragging her and staggered along northwards. Just as she came to the foot

of the mountain, a human caught sight of her: "Hey, a wolf's making off with a child!" He took out his gun to shoot her, but she lacked the strength to run and breathed her last trying to protect Kiku with her own body.

The man was surprised to find not a single bite mark on the girl's body, now quite cold. He buried her small body then and there, leaving the old she-wolf exposed to the elements at her graveside, from where, even reduced to bones, she kept watch over Kiku.

The Red Dragonfly
and the Cockroach

On a small isolated island, far to the south, an aeroplane lay on the white beach that sparkled in the summer sun.

I say "lay" because it really did look like some kind of creature sprawled out on the sand. Indeed, it gave an extremely lazy impression of gazing at the sea lost in thought, and it was hard to imagine it cutting a dashing figure up in the sky.

The plane had a two-blade propeller that was too large for its small fuselage, a clumsy-looking engine, double-tier wings, and on its side was the bold image of the Rising Sun flag.

A closer look revealed that one of its protruding legs had snapped, and one of the tail fins was torn off. Four days before, the plane had flown shakily over this island, circling forlornly like a bird looking for a branch on which to perch so that it could rest its wings, before finally summoning up the courage to land on the beach.

A normal plane would probably have sunk into the sand, burst into flames and ended up a complete wreck. As it happened, though, this was one of the basic training planes known as a "Red Dragonfly" that most people regarded with a mixture of affection and disdain. More toy-like than a regular plane, it had careened over the sand before coming to a stop with only minimal damage.

A young pilot, little more than a child himself, alighted from the cockpit. He was just eighteen years old, a fresh graduate of the Japanese Navy's preparatory pilot-training course and still inexpert at the controls. And even if his plane was an ageing Red Dragonfly, it was what Japan was using at the time for its kamikaze attacks.

At the start of the war, Japan had had the world-class Zero fighter plane and many well-trained veteran pilots who shot down many American and British planes, but from 1943 the tables turned and Japan no longer had the upper hand. It was during the Leyte operation in 1944 that pilots were first ordered to crash their planes into enemy ships to sink them in what became known as kamikaze attacks. And since there was no time to manufacture new planes, it wasn't long before they started using the Red Dragonflies.

These were effectively relics of the previous century. Not only were they slow, with the added weight of heavy bombs they even had trouble taking off. However, the Americans were initially unaware of this, and to begin with they apparently mistook the Red Dragonflies for a new weapon.

When their fighter planes like the Grumman, P-51 or Corsair, which were capable of outperforming the Zero, caught sight of a Red Dragonfly sputtering along and went in for the attack, before they knew it they had left it far behind. They were travelling so much faster that it was difficult to take aim at them, and they were convinced that Japan had managed to make a plane that could stop in mid-air.

Incidentally, there's an anecdote about an American pilot, about to engage in battle with an even more antiquated plane than the Red Dragonfly, gesturing urgently to indicate its landing gear was still down. He apparently considered it unfair to fight a plane that had forgotten to retract its landing gear, but actually it was fixed and had no means of retracting it.

To get back to the story, the young pilot had twice before boarded a kamikaze plane, received his orders to attack and gone in search of an enemy ship. Both times he'd received notification of an enemy task force at sea to the south and had gone on sortie, but not only was his Red Dragonfly slow, it was also short-range and he'd been unable to locate the enemy.

The first time he'd gone out, his

commanding officer had stood before the fledgling pilots and instructed them, "You are going to die protecting our country, which lovingly raised all of you, and your mothers and sweethearts. You are not the only ones to die, so go out in the knowledge that others will be following you, and annihilate the enemy devils!"

The youth couldn't summon much enthusiasm for the idea of dying for his country, but if it was for his mother then he would gladly do so. Every morning without fail, come snow or blazing heat, his mother had laid out her vegetable wares on top of a small box on the streets where they lived in northern Japan. Goodness only knew when she managed to sleep, for she also busied herself with odd jobs at a sake brewery, the fruit harvest and night work. His father had died young, and all they had was a piece of land the size of a postage stamp, so she had had to work hard to send him to school. Her strong arms were tanned almost black, but she was gentle and loving to him.

"For Mama!" he thought, gunning the engine, and as he heard the forlorn put-put of the propeller, barely a roar, he felt no fear at his impending death, but rather smiled. He had always depended on his mother. He had opted to go on the training course of his own free will, but he had always been sure of the unconditional presence of his strong, gentle mother somehow watching over him from a distance. Now, though, it was he who could protect her.

She would no doubt be overcome with grief when her only child was killed in action, but he thought only of his joy at being at last able to fulfil his filial duty, repaying her kindness by protecting her. This too was merely youthful conceit, although he didn't realize it at the time.

Even in the cockpit of the Red Dragonfly as it rose into the air, the youth thought only of his mother. She could take pride in him dying an honourable death as a kamikaze pilot, and with his soldier's pension she would never have to sell vegetables again. Gazing at the photograph of him, brave and smiling, surely she could live content.

He recalled the unseasoned logs smoking in the sunken hearth in the middle of their living room, and the straw-thatched roof which sucked up the smoke; and how, when it was about to rain or snow, the smoke would linger and bring tears to their eyes; and, when they made the blaze fiercer because of the cold, how he'd burnt his legs badly enough to leave scars. The youth let his thoughts wander in the past, and he could clearly hear her voice against the sound of the engine, and smell her warm scent.

The group of three Red Dragonflies flew in formation, their engines running smoothly with a light put-put sound. It hardly seemed credible that once they caught sight of the enemy they would go into a dive, and the youth would also become a component of the bomb. The sea was calm, and the shadows from the planes were clearly reflected on the surface, although of course there wasn't anything so peaceful as fishing boats anywhere in sight.

Eventually the pilot of the lead plane, accustomed to navigating over the sea, turned its nose back towards the mainland, and the youth followed. If they had carried on any farther without finding any enemy to attack, they would have crashed into the sea and the mission would have been in vain. And the Red Dragonflies were a precious military capability that couldn't be allowed to go to waste.

Arriving back at the base he had never expected to see again, the youth felt as though the past two-hour flight had been a dream. Now when he thought of his resolve to protect his mother he felt a little ashamed, but when he realized that he would have died had they found the enemy, he was gripped by such fear that his knees felt wobbly and his teeth chattered.

Upon hearing their report their commanding officer, as if he knew what the youth was thinking, instructed them irritably, "Recently, you lot seem to be lacking in spirit when out searching for the enemy. Any attack delayed by even a day just gives the enemy more time to prepare for the invasion. Martyring yourself for a good cause is the greatest opportunity for honour, never forget that."

The youth didn't think he was particularly cowardly, or prone to attacks of nerves, but it was true that he'd been the one flying the plane. It was a strange way to put it, but he had the feeling he'd been rather lax: instead of searching for enemy ships, he'd been lost in thoughts of his mother, the mountains of home, the river's winding course. Reflecting deeply on this as he returned to his quarters, he overheard two labourers about the same age as him who were working on the base.

"The kamikaze pilots have it good, they can eat and drink their fill and spend the whole day playing around."

"We'll die just the same, but squashed like bugs during the invasion."

It was true that the kamikaze pilots received special treatment on the base; the food was good, and they had a fair amount of freedom. Rather than feeling angry, the youth was ashamed that he had returned alive today. He told himself that he had to die, not to protect his country or his mother, but because it wasn't right for him to be eating eggs and tomato and sweet bean porridge every day when there was such a shortage of food.

The time for the second mission came round, and this time the commanding officer kept it short, telling them merely, "I am praying for your success. The Japanese people, indeed Japanese history, are watching your ambitious undertaking," as he waved them off.

Once again the three Red Dragonflies headed south to the tune of the put-put of the propellers under the languorous summer sun. This time the youth was wondering whether or not he would feel pain when he crashed into the enemy ship. It probably would hurt, but, then again, he might lose consciousness before the impact.

He'd heard from his seniors that the barrage of anti-aircraft fire was like the spray rebounding from a heavy shower, and even a Zero would have its wings torn off if hit by bullets from an anti-aircraft machine-gun. How much more so, then, for this little Red Dragonfly? If he was hit, would he feel a shock, or would the plane disintegrate leaving him hanging alone in mid-air?

Everyone has to die, and mine will be an honourable death in action for the sake of my country and my mother. I will become one of the devils that helped to annihilate the despicable enemy in defence of the nation, and that will together form the cornerstone of the East through the glory of our unfailing devotion to the Empire.

Since completing his training, he had often repeated these words taught to him by his instructor, but they struck him as somewhat hollow. He wondered what he would be thinking at the moment of impact. It was said your life flashed before your eyes like a kaleidoscope, but was that really true?

The sea was as calm as ever, and now and then he would hurriedly take a look around, but there was nothing in sight. Cloud cover was level two, visibility good, and moreover the youth had 20/20 vision, yet somehow it was as if there was a mist over the water blurring the pattern of waves and clouds on the surface. No, in fact he could see it clearly, but lightly floating there in the sky he felt aimless, unsure even whether he was upright or upside down, whether the expanse of sea below him was in fact sky, whether he was actually now travelling south—or perhaps he had already died and was on his way to the Yasukuni Shrine.

And again the lead pilot signalled for the three Red Dragonflies to return to base, having failed to locate the enemy. This time the youth had felt keenly afraid. The thought of his own body converted into a bomb and scattered in all directions was just so outlandish that he had rather been lulled into a dreamlike state. However, the gazes of those waiting for him as he returned alive were only too real, and he could hear them muttering amongst themselves.

"Once a guy fails a mission he gets cold feet."

"Whoever heard of a living god? Is this what the Imperial Navy has come to?"

Indeed, before he'd entered the cockpit of a suicide plane, the youth himself had looked coldly upon any pilots returning fruitlessly from a mission.

"It's nothing to worry about," the lead pilot, two years his senior and his mentor, consoled him upon returning from reporting to the commanding officer. "In any case, if you're in a Red Dragonfly, a hundred times out

of a hundred the dive-bomb will be ineffective. Even with the best planes in Japan today, the success rate is less than ten per cent. Still, you never know, we may get lucky so I'm waiting for our chance. Just follow me."

Since the kamikaze pilots were exempted from work, the youth spent all his time sprawled out on his straw mattress. If the lead pilot was right, how on earth could he summon the will to go on a mission just to die? It was all very well calling it a glorious death, but in effect all they were doing was costing the Americans a few bullets.

He lost his appetite, and was too young to drown his sorrows with alcohol. One day he found a cockroach in the mattress. He caught it and put it in a matchbox, where he could gaze at its glossy skin and touch its long, wavy whiskers with his finger. When he first saw it, he hadn't thought of keeping it, but it was still young and easy to catch. He couldn't bring himself to kill it, and instead fed it with scraps of bread and vegetables, and ended up feeling quite fond of it. He distracted himself by telling the cockroach he would take it with him on the next mission, and reassured himself with the thought that it would witness his last moments.

At length the order for the third mission was issued, and again the three Red Dragonflies set off southwards. The youth put the matchbox in his flight-suit pocket, and once he reached cruising altitude, he let the cockroach loose on his knee. It must have become accustomed to being shut up in a small space, or was perhaps affected by the altitude, for it remained unmoving. When the youth nudged it, it crawled onto his finger and sat there waving its whiskers.

What would happen after he died? The Americans would of course land on the mainland, and would probably advance to the north where his mother lived. He had seen Japanese Army personnel in the vicinity of the base. They were supposed to be the national defence guard, but they didn't have proper guns and were spending their time either building shelters or training with bamboo spears. It was obvious they didn't stand a chance of winning like that. Would all the Japanese population die? What about his mother, would she be burnt with flamethrowers as he'd heard had happened on Saipan, Iwo Jima and Okinawa, or would she kill herself first?

He didn't feel sad, or pumped up for the battle, but instead was enjoying the ticklish feeling of the cockroach as it began to crawl around. *You're the only friend I have*, he thought as he stroked its back. Its skin looked hard, but it was actually quite soft to the touch. *You've got wings, so get away before we crash*. Even if it did, though, it probably wouldn't survive out there at sea, and he felt sorry for bringing it along with him. It suddenly occurred to him that if he'd just let it be, it would now be back at the base crawling around the wall as it pleased,

eating scraps of leftover food. He began to regret having been so cruel.

Maybe all the people in Japan would be killed and Japan would be taken over by cockroaches. All the Mama, Papa and baby cockroaches would enjoy flying and crawling around the mountains and fields, and maybe that was okay.

While he'd been engrossed in his thoughts about cockroaches, he'd somehow lost sight of the other two planes and now found himself all alone hovering between the sky and sea. Shocked, he scanned the sky all around him, but he couldn't see his two companions, let alone any enemy ship.

He was acutely aware of his impending death now. How could he have lost sight of the lead plane? He had

no idea which way was which, and all he could do was carry on flying until his fuel ran out and he crashed into the sea.

Surprisingly, he didn't feel afraid. Even if he had to die like a dog, though, he wanted to let the cockroach live and decided that he would crash-land on an island if the opportunity presented itself. He strained his eyes harder, and eventually spotted land. The beach sparkled as sunlight caught on the fragments of coral mixed in with the white sand. It looked solid enough to be a runway, so he urgently sought out the widest space and manipulated the Red Dragonfly into a shaky landing.

The youth alighted from the plane with the cockroach, but the sun was beating down so fiercely that he put the cockroach back in the cockpit. He took the remains of a rice ball out of his pocket along with his flight chocolate and placed them beside it. Then he went into the forest in search of better food for it. He didn't know whether it would like the soft leaves and grasses he gathered, but perhaps it would be able to survive on them.

When he'd done all he could, the youth took off all his clothes and walked to the water's edge, where he turned back for one last look at the Red Dragonfly. It looked like a clumsy creature that had simply alighted there. Better that for a Red Dragonfly than disintegrating in mid-air engulfed in flames, he thought. Then he started swimming straight out to sea. He briefly wondered in which

direction lay the northern region where his mother lived, but immediately banished the thought and just focused on moving his arms and legs, stretching them out and pulling them in, swimming single-mindedly on and on.

On 15th August, a Red Dragonfly lay on the white sand of a southern island. In its cockpit a cockroach with glossy skin crouched waving its whiskers, as if yearning for the familiar smell of the youth.

The Prisoner of War
and the Little Girl

In the long, narrow town squeezed in between sea and mountain, numerous tunnels had been dug into the mountainside to serve as air-raid shelters. Nobody bothered to rush to the shelters any more, though, even when an air-raid warning sounded.

This was because the entire town from sea to mountain had been completely razed to the ground a couple of months before, and only a handful of people were now living in the burnt-out ruins. Now and then a B-29 would fly overhead, but even if they'd wanted to drop any bombs there wasn't anything left for them to target. All that was left was a bleak wasteland with no gas, electricity or water. You could confidently say that it was the safest place in Japan at the time.

This was how nobody noticed that a lone American had set up home deep inside one of the shelters on the mountainside. Or rather he hadn't so much set up home as, having nowhere else to go, taken refuge here. He sat hugging his knees, unaware of the passage of time from day to night and night to day, like a mole fearful of the summer light.

The American was a prisoner of war captured by the Japanese Army on 8th December 1941, soon after the start of the war. His name was Steve.

At the very beginning of the war the outlook for Japan was good, and they'd advanced throughout the southern Pacific at lightning speed, forcing American, British and Dutch forces to raise the white flag with barely a chance to return fire, and capturing many of their soldiers.

According to Western thinking, there was nothing shameful about being taken prisoner of war. On the contrary, fighting to the bitter end without fleeing, and being taken prisoner only after exhausting every available means, was seen rather as honourable. And under international treaties, POWs had the right to humane treatment, so to begin with Steve and his fellow prisoners had been quite relaxed about it all.

They were confined to a makeshift prison enclosed by a fence in a corner of the island that they had been defending. There was no chance of them escaping as they were surrounded in all directions by the ocean, and the Japanese soldiers guarding them could afford to be generous, so they all got along fairly well.

Half a year later, the POWs were taken to Japan. Japan's youth were being steadily sent to the front, so there was a lack of workers in the factories at a time when there was a need to make a lot more weapons. Students and schoolchildren were being ordered away from their studies into the factories, and not even womenfolk were allowed to remain idle, so it was unacceptable to have just the POWs languishing at their leisure.

Steve and his fellows were therefore sent to work in a steel haulage warehouse on the seafront of the long, narrow town. The forced labour of POWs was prohibited, but Japan could not afford to have full-grown men lying around idle, and the military had a rather different idea of POWs from other countries. "Never accept the shame of being taken prisoner!" they ordered their own soldiers. If they were taken prisoner they would bring disgrace not only on themselves, but on their entire family.

This way of thinking was actually quite recent. Centuries ago, in the Warring States period, for example, even if a warrior surrendered to the enemy, became his ally and fought against his former lord, he wasn't considered a traitor. Since the beginning of the Meiji period, however, Japan had been a poor island nation striving to conduct itself as a world power. To do this it had to force soldiers to go to war. Once they realized that not just they would be affected, but their parents and children would no longer be able to show their faces in public if they disgraced them, they couldn't hold their own lives too dear.

Even if they knew a battle was lost they had to charge to their deaths, and it was this brave spirit that made up for their diminished numbers and poorly armed forces. Each successive war—from the Sino-Japanese, Russo-Japanese and China-Japan wars to the Pacific War—reinforced this way of thinking in the Japanese military. If they had only forced it on their own troops it might have been okay, but they started viewing the POWs from the countries they were at war with in the same way.

The first town that Steve saw in Japan was still relatively untainted by the shadow of war, and he was relieved at how peaceful it looked. And after all, life on the small southern island had been monotonous with no women or children in sight. Arriving in port and disembarking from the ship, he felt quite relaxed and even smiled and waved at the people they passed on the way to the barracks that had been prepared as a prison.

"Look at that POW grinning like a monkey. The nerve!"

"If that's what these damned Yanks are like, they're bound to lose."

Steve and the others had no idea that the townspeople were whispering such things about them. At the same time, it was natural for the townspeople to think this way. In the early summer of 1942, a woman who had shown sympathy towards some POWs had been branded a traitor and harshly berated by the military before the entire nation.

The POWs were put to work right away. They might have been big and strong, and so were highly valued, but they were also despised in equal measure. For one thing they were considered stupid for working so hard for their enemy captors, and for another they were feared for their ability to dispatch their work far more efficiently than any of the Japanese workers.

At that time, many people had been drafted from their regular occupations into the war effort, and put to work in factories and warehouses.

Skilled craftsmen were made to push trolleys, barbers to wield hammers and clockmakers to dig holes. However, they could never throw themselves into the work, however much they were told it was for the good of their country. After all, if they injured their hands they wouldn't be able to make a living back in peacetime, and so they were very careful not to crush their fingers.

The regular workers, too, were annoyed by the military who knew nothing about the factory yet came and threw their weight around, acting as if they were the only ones doing anything for the war effort. And what's more, there was a shortage of electricity and materials. Even if ordered to work through the night, it wasn't as if they could build aeroplanes and ships on the Japanese spirit alone.

There were also some unscrupulous workers who were so fed up that on cold winter days they burned machine tools for warmth, and stole paint, wire and oil to exchange for food.

The hardest workers of them all were the POWs and also the schoolchildren, who believed that Japan would definitely win the war as they'd been taught at school. Steve and his fellow POWs were increasingly given the toughest jobs, while their food rations became more and more meagre by the day, although this was true for everyone.

They were all reduced to skin and bones, with just their eyes bulging, but never for a moment did any of them ever doubt that America would win the war. They had been completely shocked when they were first taken prisoner in an ambush, and were so impressed by Japan's Zero fighter planes that they thought Japan must be an incredibly strong country. Once they saw the reality on the mainland, however, they felt almost disappointed.

Just about all the machinery had been manufactured in America or Britain, and most of that was so old it wouldn't be out of place in a museum. All the factory workers were sickly, and they still used horses and cows to transport materials. On the whole they were rather to be pitied.

The POWs were never given any news but, piecing things together from what they happened to see around town, they could get a general idea of how things were going. People were beginning to construct air-raid shelters on the roadsides, and their clothing was becoming more and more ragged, while the soldiers guarding them were replaced by increasingly doddery old men.

"Looks like Japan's finished, eh?"

"I'm already dreaming of ice cream floats..."

"Wonder what's happening in the baseball league?"

"I don't want to see another grain of rice as long as I live!"

They all felt homesick, and fervently longed for the day when the Allies would land in Japan and rescue them.

Then, in the late autumn of 1944, the B-29s began flying reconnaissance missions. Steve and his fellows cheered loudly at the magnificent sight of a plane trailing a cloud as it flew west to east over the town, only to be berated by their irritated guards.

"Let them drop their bombs! We'll make sure you lot are right underneath."

"We'll execute ten of you for every Japanese they kill."

They knew these were just empty threats, but nevertheless they felt a twinge of discomfort knowing that their factory was producing weapons and could very well be targeted by the Allies. If they were in Europe they might consider escaping, but in Japan they had nowhere to escape to. As the day of victory drew closer, if anything their unease grew.

At the start of 1945 the air raids finally began in earnest. Steve and the others were strictly confined to the factory to prevent them from sending signals to the B-29s, but otherwise they weren't treated any more harshly in retaliation for the attacks.

One night in early summer the town was hit by an air raid for the second time. The first time the POWs had clapped their hands and cheered, but this time incendiary bombs rained down all around them. There was no shelter in the prison, but ironically the guards consoled them, "Don't worry, those B-types know you're here, don't they? We'll be okay."

That might be so, but if the flames reached them they would have no means to get away, so the POWs searched desperately for an escape route. As they were doing so, a small bomb fell right next to them and blew a hole in the prison fence.

They ran out through it but, surrounded by flames, they didn't know which way to run. Even if they did manage to escape the blaze, they'd probably be lynched by townspeople whose houses had burnt down. Some ran for the sea, and others returned to the prison. Steve went off on his own in search of refuge.

Soon the entire area was razed to the ground and was like a dreamscape, with fires glowing like fireflies all over. He didn't meet a soul as he walked the streets. It was the first time in years he had been unsupervised, and he became quite carried away roaming around. By the time he came to his senses, he had reached the foothills.

And as the fires were finally extinguished and darkness fell, people began appearing here and there. Steve suddenly felt afraid, like a child who had become separated from his mother at a festival. But even if he wanted to return to the prison, he didn't know how.

He lay down on a gentle slope and thought to himself that it would be fine if the night would never end, but before long the sky in the east grew light. Looking down at the town he saw that not a single building was left standing. Everything had burnt down. But there was no time to feel either shocked or happy at the Allied forces' success. The military police and civil guard must be out and about, and already aware that the POWs had escaped.

For the time being, Steve sneaked into one of the abandoned tunnel shelters. As long as he was in a darkish place, he could feel at ease. He recalled playing in old gold mines as a child, fascinated by the damp air in the shafts, despite his mother scolding him that they were dangerous.

"Mama!" he murmured. He felt as scared and helpless as a child.

As if in answer, a girl appeared and, sobbing, cried out as he had done, "Mama!"

Steve was about to make a run for it, but then realized that she was only about six or seven years old. She looked so sad that he asked her, "Hey, what's up?"

Of course he spoke in English, but the little girl seemed to understand, for she sobbed, "Mama's gone."

Steve didn't know any Japanese, but he understood her perfectly. "Cheer up!" he said, stroking her hair. "She'll be back soon."

"No, she won't. She's dead, and our house burnt down."

Steve was at a loss how to comfort her. Hundreds or even thousands of people must have burnt to death in those flames. The little girl didn't seem to have any qualms about Steve being American, and she sat quietly beside him clutching her doll.

If he stayed here, it would only be a matter of time before he was discovered. On the other hand, he couldn't just abandon the little girl. Most importantly, he had to find food and water. The war would soon be over, and he wanted to stay alive until then. He glanced around, wishing that he had a pair of wings.

"Um, there's a bigger shelter farther up," the little girl told him, as if reading his mind.

When he went to check it out, he found that it extended much farther back into the mountain, and was well kitted out with emergency food rations. That in itself meant that people would surely come, but if he hid himself away right at the back, nobody was likely to notice anyone there in the darkness unless they were specifically looking.

Steve and the girl decided to make their nest there. The girl's father had been a pilot, and had died in battle two years before, so she was an orphan.

"When the war ends, I'll take you to America with me."

"America? But that's a bad country isn't it?"

"No, no, it really isn't."

And so he did his best to describe America to her. As he told her about the wide open plains, deserts, huge rivers, skyscrapers and cars everywhere, pieces of the life he'd once led in America all those years before began coming back to him.

Everyone from the ruined town had fled to the countryside, and nobody came to check up on the air-raid shelters. In all the chaos, even if one of the POWs had gone missing, they'd probably assumed he'd been burnt to death. Many people must have been reduced to mere lumps of charcoal, and an American body would be indistinguishable from a Japanese one.

Steve and the little girl became as close as brother and sister. From time to time she would go down to the spring to fetch water in a charred bucket. When at night she cried for her mother, Steve would hold her close and sing her to sleep with American lullabies. The war seemed far away, and the two of them thought only of going to America.

And then it was the 15th of August. The girl went to fetch water as usual, and happened to overhear an elderly couple passing by say angrily, "The war's over. Japan lost."

"What? Is the war over?" asked the girl. She didn't really know what this

meant, but if it was true then she'd be able to go to America. That's what Steve was always telling her. "Well, I guess I can go to America, then."

"Don't be silly, America's coming here."

"No, no—my friend said he'd take me to America!"

Wondering what she was talking about, the old man questioned her further, and finally realized that there must be an American POW hiding in the old air-raid shelters.

Now that they had lost to America, it might cause problems if it became known they'd been mistreating POWs. He rushed to tell the military police and the local policeman, who were quite taken aback and decided to go and fetch him.

Hearing the noise of the big procession making its way to the mountainside, and not knowing the war had ended, Steve thought he'd finally been discovered and immediately took to his heels, heading into the mountains at a sprint.

"Hey, the war's over! We can go to America!" the little girl called after him in Japanese, but Steve could no longer understand her.

"The war's over. It's ended!" called out the townspeople in unison.

But Steve ran deeper and deeper into the mountains, as if pursued by their voices, and that was the last anyone ever saw of him.

The Cake Tree
in the Ruins

Two months after the B-29s firebombed the town, the ruins had been taken over by rampant weeds. There was no longer any prospect of any more air raids, so the people living in the shelters or makeshift shacks, constructed from corrugated iron balanced over any walls left standing, were looking altogether more cheerful.

Immediately after everything had burnt down, schoolchildren had been out retrieving pieces of metal and patching up the roadside shelters, so that the ruins had been tidied up after a fashion. Now, though, they were lying neglected once again. When it rained, water ran through the streets gouging out the soil into mini-ravines and forming small lakes, and causing the shelters to cave in. With the weeds running riot over everything, it was hard to believe that this had once been a densely populated town.

Families in these ruins lived like primitives, scavenging for any pieces of charred wood that could be used as fuel, and fetching seawater from the beach. Of course there was no electricity, so once the sun went down all they could do was sleep.

Depending on your perspective this could be considered a very healthy lifestyle, but then there was no escaping the lack of food. Daily rations had been reduced from 350g to 320g and consisted not of rice but of defatted soy flour or maize, and even then usually arrived late.

It was possible to purchase food in the countryside, but everything had been destroyed in the fires so nobody had anything to offer in exchange. Even if you did have any money it was hardly worth the paper it was printed on, while workmen's outfits were in high demand—rubber-soled split-toed boots, work gloves, gaiters, that sort of thing.

Adults were better at enduring these conditions, but it was really tough on growing children, especially since it was the grown-ups who had gone to war in the first place while the children were simply innocent victims. For those children between the ages of five and ten in 1945, it really was a miserable existence—they had never eaten anything tasty, while however hungry the grown-ups were now they could remember eating their fill of delicious food in the past.

They would reminisce about the tasty eel in such-and-such a restaurant, and the mouth-watering tempura in another, especially the shrimp and vegetable fritters. Having really indulged themselves in the past, now that life was a bit tough they could reconcile themselves to going without.

However, the children didn't even have memories to sustain themselves with. Rice had been rationed since 1941, sugar was hard to come by, the cakes and candies that had once flooded into the ports had vanished, and by the end of the war the only sweets available were dried bananas and sweet potatoes.

In order to survive, the children formed gangs to go scavenging for the tomatoes, cucumbers, pumpkins and other vegetables people had started growing in the ruins. They knew it was wrong to steal, but survival was more important to them, and they could sniff out exactly where tomatoes were turning red or pumpkins were swelling up nicely.

"Hey, what's this tree?"

One day, they came across a single tree growing vigorously amidst the ruins. While the weeds were flourishing, all the trees had been burnt down and any that had somehow escaped the worst of the flames had been cut down for firewood, so it was quite impossible for there to be any healthy trees left standing. Yet this tree was full of vitality, stretching its leafy branches up to the blue sky. Indeed, it seemed to be growing before their very eyes.

"Why here?"

"This is where that big house once was. I used to come here to collect cicadas."

"But everything must have burnt down."

"There were a lot of trees in the garden. It must be one of those."

"But the leaves aren't even a little bit dried up."

Some trees surrounding a shrine a short distance from the ruins had survived, but all their leaves had been scorched by the heat from the flames. Yet the leaves on this mysterious tree in the ruins of the big old house seemed to be sprouting one after another with fresh green growth.

"Mmm. It smells nice."

"Yeah, and those leaves look quite tasty."

"Don't be silly, since when did anyone ever eat tree leaves?"

The children all knew as well as any botanist what plants they could or couldn't eat, but they had never heard of tree leaves being edible, however tasty they might look. Well, apart from persimmon leaves, which were dried to make a flour that tasted slightly sweet.

One of the boys reached out and grabbed a leaf from the mysterious tree and crammed it into his mouth. He munched on it for a moment and then exclaimed loudly, "Waaah! Yum!" The boy who had been so sure that tree leaves were inedible also picked off a leaf and put it his mouth, then all of a sudden all the children were scrambling up the tree and hanging off branches to get at the leaves. A branch snapped off, releasing a sweet fragrance. The children were stunned.

"Hey, look at that!" said one, pointing at the place where the branch had broken. The age rings were clearly visible, as they should be, but strangely the sweet smell seemed to be emanating from just that point.

"It's soft!"

"Soft?"

"Yes, soft."

He touched the tree and then put his finger in his mouth, and was instantly transfixed. Seeing this, the others all wordlessly followed suit, timorously touching the scar on the tree trunk and then licking their fingers. It was soft and sweet.

When they finally came to their senses, they realized this soft sweetness on their tongues was unlike anything they had ever tasted before. Everything they had eaten until now had felt coarse in their mouths, and had tasted salty. Boiled wheat bran dumplings felt like sand, defatted soy was just like gravel, and there really were often little bits of grit mixed in with the rice gruel.

All the children started breaking off branches and gobbling them up. The tree looked just like any other ordinary tree with hard branches, but the moment they put a piece into their mouths, it melted on their tongues and an indescribably sweet taste spread through their entire bodies.

"This must be a bread tree," said one.

They had all read about a tree in the South Seas that had bread as its fruit, which the local people could eat to their hearts' content, and they had all thought how wonderful it would be to have such a tree in Japan. However, this tree wasn't a bread tree—far from it. Bread was a real treat for these children, even if the only bread they'd ever tasted was black and went off really quickly. This tree, though, was far, far sweeter. It couldn't possibly be bread.

"Maybe it's a cake tree."

"A cake tree?"

All of the children had forgotten what cake was—or rather they had never even known. They had only heard about it from the old women, who muttered things like, "You poor darlings. In the old days we had things like sponge cake, and bean jelly, but you've never had a chance to eat such treats, have you?"

"Is that what it is? I had no idea cake was so scrumptious!"

And even though a moment ago they had thought they were fit to burst, they suddenly felt hungry again and broke off some more branches. And however many branches they snapped off, the tree remained as thick and bushy as ever.

The old house the children were talking about had been the biggest in the whole area. A sickly boy of eight had lived there alone with his mother, having lost his Papa early on. They were rich and, had it not been for the war, they wouldn't have lacked for anything. When food became scarce, his mother would go all over town in search of provisions. Being a sickly child, he would get a terrible tummy ache and come out in a rash after eating the coarse food they received on rations.

His mother took his late Papa's clothes to the countryside to exchange them for rice, and to the coast where she could get fish. However, everyone knows that sweet fare provides the best nourishment for sickly children, cake being the most effective of all, and so she went to great lengths to acquire wheat flour, eggs and sugar. Recalling the taste and fragrance of the cakes they had enjoyed together with Papa, she turned her hand to baking.

She also pulled strings to acquire extra ingredients like caramel and chocolate. By this time, the sweets that had been available to all children in peacetime were reserved for the military. This was understandable, since caramels were the best for sustaining soldiers exhausted from the fierce fighting, and chocolate was distributed to pilots to help keep them awake.

When his mother managed to get hold of some chocolate, she would spread it melted on bread and decorate it like a proper cake before giving it to her son to eat. She would dig out old magazines and follow their recipes to make sponge cakes, cream puffs and pies. She wasn't a very good cook, but the boy appreciated her efforts and joyfully ate the burnt cakes and cream puff shells that tasted of soap.

But she wanted her son to be able to taste all the cookies, pound cakes, eclairs, rum babas and other cakes she remembered eating long ago. And then she heard rumours that the German manager of an old cake shop had decided, now that he would inevitably be put out of business once the firebombing started, to make his last ever cake for his customers to enjoy. It was as if he'd read her mind! She rushed out to the shop.

Of course it was a secret and he was only sharing the cake with the customers who had been with him since before the war. Upon hearing her desperate pleas, however, the baker's plump wife sold her a piece with a kindly smile and said, "Don't worry, we'll all be able to eat such delicacies again one day."

The cake was a Baumkuchen, with layers that resembled the growth rings on a tree. Even before the war, Baumkuchen had been rather hard to find, so Mama was overjoyed to take some home to her son. "This cake really looks like a tree, doesn't it? But it's so delicious!" she told him, remembering the time she had eaten it with Papa in a cake shop in Karuizawa. It had come with a dollop of cream then, but that was out of the question now when it was impossible even to find milk.

"It lasts for a very long time, so let's take our time over eating it." She gave the boy a little piece every day, almost as if it were medicine. The way things were going, she never knew what was going to happen next, but she felt a little better now that her son had at last been able to taste something truly exquisite.

And when at length they were down to the very last piece, instead of eating it the boy decided to save it. He emptied out the box where he kept all his treasures—things like a marble, a sword guard and the spring from a clock—and put the piece of Baumkuchen in there. Every now and then he would secretly open it up and smell the deliciously sweet fragrance that never faded, and it always revived the delicious taste for him. After three months the piece of cake was quite dry and had begun to break up into hard little crumbs, but still the fragrance remained undiminished.

And eventually the air-raid warning sounded. The mother ushered her son into the shelter in the garden and told him, "You'll be safe as long as you're in here. I have to look after the house." He watched as she went back to the house, looking brave in her air-raid hood and baggy work trousers, a bucket hanging from one arm. He never saw her again.

She perished in the flames that swept through the town. The shelter in the garden became very hot inside, but the boy survived and, when everything had fallen quiet, he fearfully poked his head outside and looked around. Nothing was left. It never occurred to him that his mother might be dead, though, and so he waited for her inside the shelter.

Whenever he felt lonely or hungry, he would gaze at the crumbs of

Baumkuchen, now black with mould. As he smelt the faint, sweet fragrance, he could feel the warm softness of his mother's skin.

She had told him that Baumkuchen was a German word that meant "cake tree". He wondered rapturously what a cake tree would be like. Did it have chocolate flowers? Maybe its fruit would be cream puffs. And then it occurred to him that the stale crumbs in his box were like seeds. He remembered seeing his mother planting flower seeds in the garden, and so he dug some holes in the earthen floor of the shelter and carefully planted a crumb in each.

The mice and lizards and other little creatures that had come to the shelter to escape the flames all seemed to be hungry, and had curled up around the boy, hardly moving. "If this cake tree grows big, I'll give you all some," he told them.

Every day he watered the seeds and waited for them to sprout. Then, after so many days had passed, the earthen floor began to bulge and swell, and a small sprout popped out. "Yes! It's sprouted! It's a cake tree!" the boy cried in delight. It was just a tiny shoot, but it instantly filled the shelter with a sweet fragrance.

As he watched, the little sprout grew taller and formed leaves. He couldn't take his eyes off it. It really was a cake tree, but at the same time it reminded him of his mother and he couldn't bring himself to eat it.

As the cake tree grew from a sapling into a mature tree, beside its roots in the shelter the little boy died. Eventually the shelter too collapsed, leaving just the magnificent tree soaring up into the summer sky.

None of the children who came across the mysterious tree in the garden of the old house ever knew the story of how it came into being. Keeping it secret from the grown-ups, they would gather round it daily and eat their fill. However many branches they tore off, it always grew more and was ever thick with leaves.

On 15th August, the war the grown-ups had started finally ended. The whole of Japan had been burnt to the ground and everyone was hungry, but amidst the ruins stood just one cake tree. It was always surrounded by children gorging themselves on its delicious leaves and branches, but the grown-ups passed right by without ever even noticing it was there.

PUSHKIN CHILDREN'S BOOKS

Just as we all are, children are fascinated by stories. From the earliest age, we love to hear about monsters and heroes, romance and death, disaster and rescue, from every place and time.

We created Pushkin Children's Books to share these tales from different languages and cultures with younger readers, and to open the door to the wide, colourful worlds these stories offer.

From picture books and adventure stories to fairy tales and classics, and from fifty-year-old bestsellers to current huge successes abroad, the books on the Pushkin Children's list reflect the very best stories from around the world, for our most discerning readers of all: children.